E
AD

Adams, Adrienne

A Halloween
happening

DATE DUE			
AG 7 '89	NO 16 '90	OC 28 '91	JY 6 '93
OC 10 '89	JA 23 '91	NO 12 '9	AG 1 6 '93
OC 23 '89	FE 12 '91	DE 1 '9	OC 1 '93
JA 29 '9	MR 19 '91	AP 2 '92	OC 19 '93
AP 3 '90	AP 20 '91	JY 2 '9	NO 3 '93
JE 25 '90	MY 14 '9	NOV 1 6 '9	DEC 15 '93
JY 13 '90	JE 25 '91	AG 27 '92	APR 2 '94
JY 19 '90	JY 5 '9	SE 18 '92	AUG 8 '94
JY 24 '90	JY 26 '91	OC 8 '9	AUG 2 0 '94
AG 21 '90	AG 16 '9	OC 17 '9	OCT 17 '9
SE 18 '90	SE 12 '9	NOV 16 '94	
OC 9 '90		MY 1 1 '93	
OC 16 '90	OC 7 '9		JAN 01 '95

201-9500   PRINTED IN U.S.A.

JUN 1 3 '96   SEP 2 0 '95

OCT 21 '95

NOV 1 4 '95

© THE BAKER & TAYLOR CO.

A HALLOWEEN HAPPENING

A
HALLOWEEN
HAPPENING

by Adrienne Adams

Charles Scribner's Sons
New York

Copyright © 1981 Adrienne Adams

Library of Congress Cataloging in Publication Data
Adams, Adrienne.   A Halloween happening.
Summary: A group of children are invited to a real
witches' Halloween celebration.
[1. Halloween—Fiction.   2. Witches—Fiction]
I. Title.
PZ7.A194Hal   [E]   81-8969
ISBN 0-684-17166-X   AACR2
This book published simultaneously in the
United States of America and in Canada—
Copyright under the Berne Convention
All rights reserved. No part of this book
may be reproduced in any form without the
permission of Charles Scribner's Sons.

1 3 5 7 9 11 13 15 17 19 RD/C 20 18 16 14 12 10 8 6 4 2

Printed in the United States of America

To
Jodie Vicenta Jacobson

"All right, everybody. It's nearly dark. Time to wake up."

"You mean *get* up. Do you realize that it's almost Halloween again, and we haven't made any plans?"

"It's getting harder all the time. There are more and more *people* around. They don't understand us."

"Well, their children do."

"Then let's invite *children* here on Halloween night. We'll give them a real *witches'* party."

"We could build something with all these pumpkins here in the field."

"How about a tall tower around a high tree?"

"*Wild* idea! I *love* it!"

"And let's see—food. We'll make toad tarts, scrambled lizard eggs, wart soup, worm waffles—all the *special* delicious things. Oh, and lots of candy bats."

"*Nothing* is too good for children."

"But first comes the tower. We'll put a big platform on top for takeoffs and landings. After all, the most exciting thing for the children will be to ride on our new bat-wing gliders. Even *we* get goose pimples from that."

"Can we do all that work?"

"Sure! I'm only a hundred and forty-nine."

"That's going fine. But more pumpkins! Hundreds more."

"Coming.—Oh, my aching back!"

"When we cut the tree limbs, let's make steps out of some of them for the inside of the tower."

"Right. The rest of the limbs can hold the building up and make the platform stronger."

"The climb through the inside we'll make very scary, with weird lights and magic mirrors and horrible music and noises."

"Now, who is that up there, playing around the sky? Tell them to come down here and get to work."

"It's getting late. The children will be here soon."

"Set those pumpkin lanterns along the path. Make them *glow* with light. People don't see in the dark as we do."

"Start the bonfire. Make a big one! Blow it! Fan it! Make it roar!"

"Bring out the food treats! Light up the tower—. There! How does everything look?"

"Beautiful! How did we *do* it?"

"Hey, this is scary!"

"Well, silly, it's *supposed* to be scary—Halloween and witches and all that stuff."

"Yes, but the invitation didn't tell us they were going to scare us to *death*!"

"I'm not scared to death—only halfway, and it's fun."

"Well, my costume is supposed to scare *them*. I wonder if it will."

"If you really want to terrify them, just take off your costume and look like *you*."

"Nee-yeh. Ver-ry funny."

"Look at that!"

"Everybody looks friendly."

"I wonder if they can talk."

"Let's find out. Hi! Thanks for the invitation!"

"Welcome to our woggle. Welcome to Halloween!"

"I thought I knew what Halloween is—but whew! I've never *seen* Halloween before!"

"I'm Wanda Witch, and it makes us happy to hear you say that. So fill up with goodies, and then explore the tower. Go all the way to the top for the *main* event. You'll be surprised."

Mmmm! This is yummy food.

"I wonder what it *is*."

"The only thing I know is, the candy bats are really candy."

"I know. I ate some. But what is everything else?"

"Who cares?"

"Well, I never *tasted* anything so good."

"Think we should eat only a little bit? We might turn into witches, ourselves!"

"Hey, maybe I'd *like* that!"

"Whew, we've been climbing for about a month! Isn't it wild?"

"I'm scared!"

"Watch your feet. It's a long tumble down there."

"That's what scares me. But I wouldn't turn back for *any*thing."

"We're nearly to the top."

"Now for a ride in space with the bat-wing gliders! All aboard as they land on the platform. One witch and one passenger. Fasten the belt. Don't bother to hold your breath—it won't help a bit. Just think, *Up! Up!*"

"*Up! UP!*"

"Well, you didn't have to *scream* it! But it worked, didn't it? Blow, wind! *Blow!*"

"Ya-a-ay!"

"Now think, *Higher! HIGHER!* Yell it if you must."

"Highest!" the children yelled. "*Highest!* It's working!"

"Hang on tight, now," Wanda Witch shouted. "Let's do some aerobatics."

"Up and up and over and over and around and 'round and 'round!" she chanted.

"We're with witches," the children kept reminding themselves as they held their breath.

Suddenly Wanda said, "Sssh! Listen! Can you hear the silence?"

"All over the sky!"

"SHUSH, NOW, EVERYBODY! Let's *make* some silence."

"S-s-s-sh!"

"This party is the greatest thing that *ever* happened to *any*body! What a shame we had to promise to be home at bedtime."

"How can we say thanks?"

"You just did!" Wanda Witch said from overhead. "We thank *you* for coming. You made us very happy."

The children looked back.

"Tha-a-anks a zillion! Goo-ood night!" they called out to the witches.

Wanda Witch called from high up, "Next year—same time—same place."

"YA-A-A-AY!"